Where Are You Going, Little Mouse?

by **Robert Kraus**

pictures by **Jose Aruego**
and **Ariane Dewey**

Greenwillow Books
An Imprint of **HarperCollins***Publishers*

The artwork was prepared as black pen-and-ink
line drawings that were combined with full-color
paintings. The typeface is Avant Garde Gothic.

Where Are You Going, Little Mouse?
Text copyright © 1986 by Robert Kraus
Illustrations copyright © 1986 by Jose Aruego and Ariane Dewey
Manufactured in China All rights reserved.
www.harperchildrens.com

Library of Congress Cataloging-in-Publication Data
Kraus, Robert, (date).
Where are you going, little mouse?
"Greenwillow Books."
Summary: A little mouse runs away from home to find
a "nicer" family, but when darkness comes, he misses
them and realizes how much he loves them.
ISBN 0-688-08747-7 (pbk.)
1. Children's stories, American.   (1. Mice—Fiction.
2. Runaways—Fiction.)   I. Aruego, Jose, ill.
II. Dewey, Ariane, ill.   III. Title
PZ7.K868Wh   1985   (E)   84-25868

For Bruce,

Billy,

Pamela,

Mary Anne,

and

Parker

—R. K.

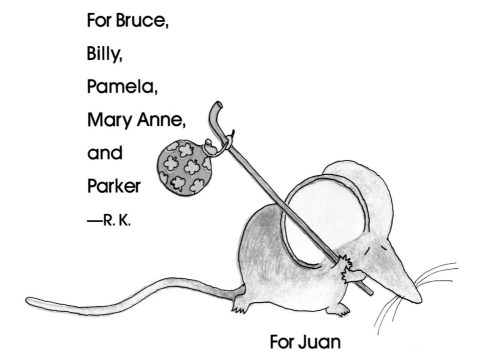

For Juan

—J. A. and A. D.

Where are you going, little mouse?

As far from home as I can go.

What of your mother?
What of your father?

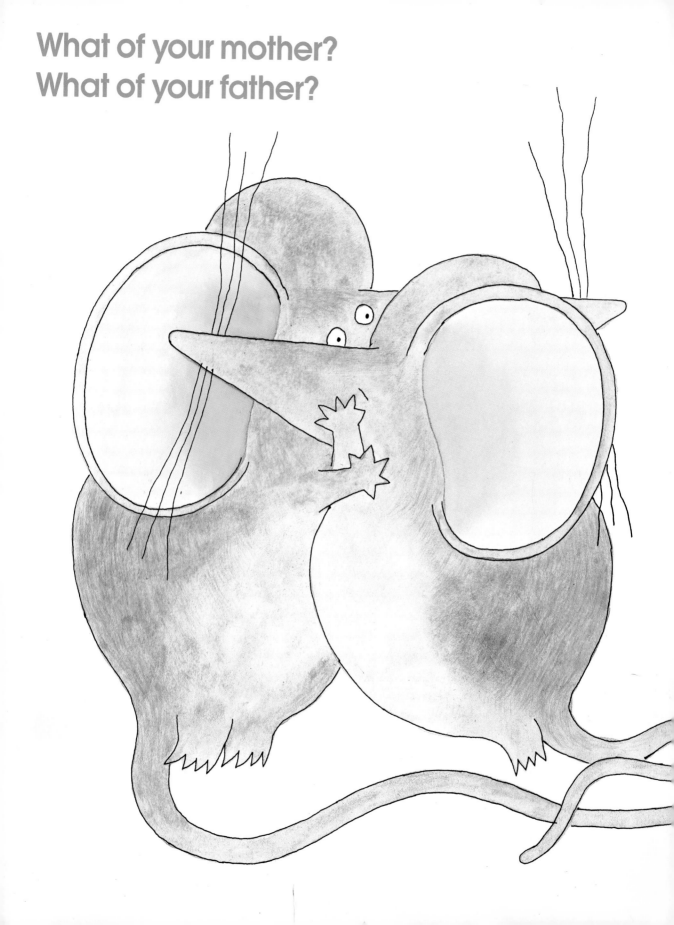

They don't love me.
They won't miss me.

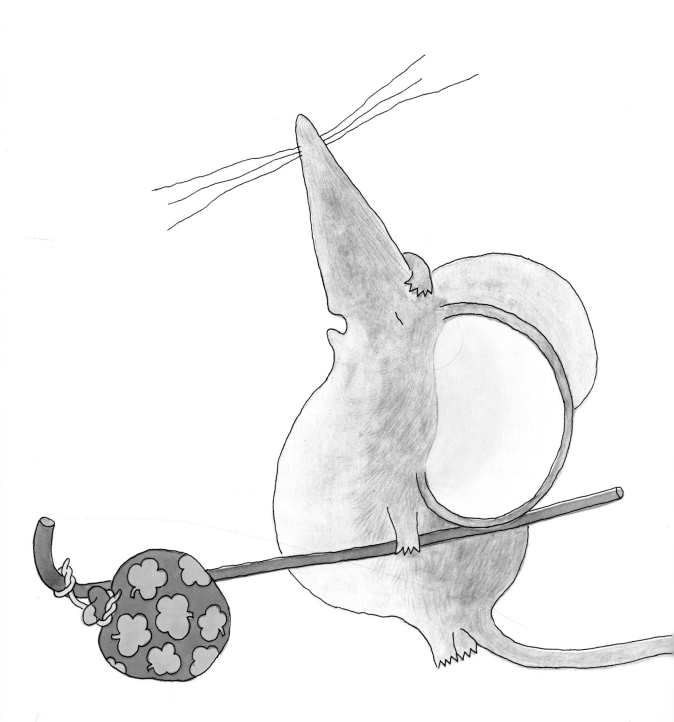

What will you do?

Find a new father who plays with me.

Find a new mother who stays with me.

Find a new brother who isn't mean.

He ~~will~~ wants to play in the tub

Find a new sister.
We're a team.

play
dress
up

I'm still looking…
I miss my mother.

I'm exploring...
I miss my father.

I'm still searching...
I miss my sister.

It's getting dark.
What will you do?

Make a phone call.

Mother, Father,
please don't worry.
Come and get me.
Hurry, hurry.

By the way
they kiss and hug me,
I can tell
they really love me.
I love them, too.

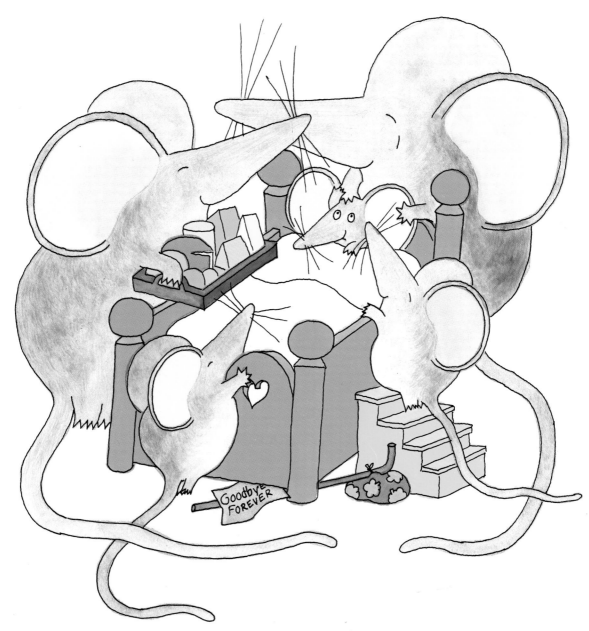